George Stuart Collins

Dryden's Dramatic Theory and Praxis

George Stuart Collins

Dryden's Dramatic Theory and Praxis

ISBN/EAN: 9783337342128

Printed in Europe, USA, Canada, Australia, Japan

Cover: Foto ©Andreas Hilbeck / pixelio.de

More available books at **www.hansebooks.com**

DRYDEN'S DRAMATIC
THEORY AND PRAXIS.

INAUGURAL DISSERTATION

FOR THE

DEGREE OF DOCTOR OF PHILOSOPHY

SUBMITTED TO THE

PHILOSOPHICAL FACULTY

OF THE

UNIVERSITY OF LEIPZIG

BY

GEORGE STUART COLLINS.

LEIPZIG - REUDNITZ
PRINTED BY OSWALD SCHMIDT.
1892.

DEDICATED

TO

MY MOTHER.

John Dryden occupies, in his capacity of *critic*, an almost unique place in the history of English literature up to his time, and his fame as an author has always rested very largely thereon. This position cannot be better characterized than in the words of Bobertag; *

"Dryden ist einer der ersten modernen dichter, in deren wirken und schaffen sich die theorie als etwas für sich existirendes, sozusagen als eine selbständige macht kundgiebt." Even the style of these critical writings is worthy of attention, since we find in them, as has more than once been noticed, "the first pieces of good modern English prose." ** Dryden possessed by no means, however, all the qualities necessary to make a great critic, nor is it at all times easy to perceive on which side of the question he is arguing, and one or two of the few opinions which we can with security accept as being his own convictions underwent, as we shall see, a radical change in a comparatively short space of time. His critical conclusions on the subject of the drama have been almost without influence on contemporary or later dramatic productions; and give, besides, in many cases, the impression of having been drawn more to justify the plays he had himself written, or intended to write, than from a desire to arrive at truth. This latter point will appear with greater clearness when we come to examine his dramatic praxis as it agrees with, or forms a contrast to, his theoretical dicta.

---

* "Dryden's Theorie des Dramas" in Kölbing's Englische Studien, Vol. IV, pp. 375, 376.
** Arnold, in the Preface to his edition of the Essay of Dramatic Poesy; Oxford, 1889.

An attempt to gather together what can be considered as Dryden's own convictions on the subject of dramatic art (by which is intended, above all, such rules as he thought should obtain in the composition of plays) and a comparison of these with the technique of his own dramas is the object of the following pages; which, it is hoped, may prove of some value as a contribution to the labors of others in the now busy field of Dryden Philology. I restrict myself to Dryden's individual opinions (as far as these are determinable) which, however, are to be arrived at only by analyses (which here follow) of such of his theoretical writings as stand in direct connection with the above mentioned purpose.

PART FIRST

DRYDEN'S DRAMATIC THEORIES.

I.

The Dedication to the Comedy "The Rival-Ladies"; published in 1664. (Edition,* Vol. II, p. 129, seq.)

In this, Dryden touches for the first time upon the question of Rhyme *versus* Blank Verse in the drama. His reasons for the preference of rhyme as stated in the above mentioned Dedication, may be summed up as follows;

a) He is not the first to employ rhyme and cannot, therefore, be accused of acting without precedent; for we find it employed in the tragedy of "Gorboduc." **

b) Rhyme is employed by the writers of "the most polished and civilized nations of Europe."***

c) The only inconvenience of rhyme is that it is not easy, in its use, to avoid closing the lines with verbs; which brings about, often, an inversion of the natural construction; But one with a good command of English will not often "be forced upon this rock."

---

* The edition used is that by Walter Scott, revised by Saintsbury: Edinburgh, 1882, seq.
** In this drama, however, only the choruses are in rhymed verse; the remainder is in blank verse.
*** Passages in quotation marks are, when no authority is cited, Dryden's own words.

d) Rhyme is said to be unnatural, but it is "only so when the poet either makes a vicious choice of words, or places them, for rhyme sake, so unnaturally as no man would in ordinary speaking."

e) Rhyme, "when judiciously ordered, has all the advantages of prose besides its own."

f) It is a help to memory; as Sir Philip Sidney shows in his "Defense of Poesy."

g) It has "in the quickness of repartee, so particular a grace".

h) "It bounds and circumscribes the fancy" — "That which most regulates the fancy and gives the judgment its busiest employment, is like to bring forth the richest and clearest thoughts"; which answers the objection — "that rhyme is only an embroidery of sense, to make that which is ordinary in itself, pass for excellent with less examination."

A proper subject must be chosen for verse, and the "argument, characters and persons must be great and noble." (In this we see the first indications of a plea for the so-called "heroic drama.") He considers as proper subjects for clothing in rhyme; "scenes of argumentation and discourse, on the result of which the doing or not doing some considerable action should depend."

II.

"*An Essay of Dramatic Poesy*"; first published in 1668, (possibly in 1667).

This is a piece of remarkably vigorous, at times elegant, prose, in the form of a discussion between the author and three of his friends; each of the four being characterized by an appropriate pseudonym. We find, as regards the purpose of this paper, four questions in reference to the drama debated,* namely:

---

* Cf. Arnold's Ed., preface, p. VII.

a) The value of the modern drama as opposed to that of the Greeks and Romans;

b) The superiority or inferiority of the French drama of the period of the Essay to the English;

c) Whether or not a drama is more perfect according to its degree of conformance to the so-called Unities; and

d) Whether rhyme or blank verse should be employed in serious plays.

A thorough analysis of this Essay would lead too far; and it may, besides, be assumed that it is known to most students of English literature, and so I confine myself to as concise a summary as possible. The author states, in the Prefatory note "To the Reader",[*] that "the drift of the discourse was chiefly to vindicate the honour of our English writers, from the censure of those who unjustly prefer the French before them": As this defence is taken up by the person called Neander, we are justified in supposing that his arguments represent Dryden's own convictions. We are also at liberty to assume, from internal evidence, that Dryden concurs in the stand taken by Eugenius[**] upon the first question; for Neander does not take exceptions to the arguments advanced by Eugenius; nor does he continue the dispute in favor of Crites,[***] who had urged the other side. Proceding upon these hypotheses, Dryden's own opinions, as expressed in the essay, would be as follows;

— In regard to a) — The modern drama excels the ancient; for the former has the benefit of the experience of the latter, but does not "draw after its lines, but those of nature"; ✔

Greek dramatic poetry was not divided into any certain number of acts;

The plots of the ancient dramas were worn so threadbare that the spectators knew the wh le action of the play from the beginning;

---

* Arnold's Ed., p. 7.
** Who represents Lord Buckhurst, according to the accepted theory of all editors.
*** Sir Robert Howard.

The Unities of Time, Place and Action are often neglected in the ancient drama;

"Instead of punishing vice, and rewarding virtue, they [the Ancients] have often shown[2] a prosperous wickedness, and an unhappy piety";

The Ancients are inferior in wit;

The ancient poets dealt with passions "which were more capable of raising horror than compassion in an audience, leaving love untouched."

In regard to b) — The French contrive their plots more regularly and observe, in general, more exactly the laws of comedy and "the decorum of the stage;" but fail in that "lively imitation of nature," which the disputants had settled upon as one of the essentials of a drama;

The French have taken up the style of drama called tragi-comedy since the death of Richelieu, in imitation of the English; but even here there is a lack of variety;*

The French plots are barren; being single, with one design only; whereas the English plays have "besides the main design, under-plots or by-concernments" which, however, all bear a relation to the principal plot. This variety, if well managed, will give greater pleasure to an audience, than one single design;

The long speeches of the French plays are cold, without development of passion. The short speeches and replies of English plays are (at least with English audiences) "more apt to move the passions and beget concernment";

The French plays contain only one character of importance; but this is no great advantage, since the well-managed introduction of persons of secondary im-

---

* In connection with the above, Dryden (i. e. Neander) defends tragi-comedy on the ground that the mirthful element is a relief to a spirit "too much bent by continual gravity." He praises tragi-comedy as a peculiar merit of the English nation, which has "invented, increased and perfected a more pleasant way of writing for the stage, than was ever known to the ancients or moderns of any nation."

portance adds to the variety of the plot and to that
pleasure experienced in following "a labyrinth of design";

The French have reason on their side when they
prefer the narration of combats and tumults to a representation of such on the stage: But the English public
desires the actual representation, nor does this neces-
sarily disturb the illusion; for one "can with as great
ease persuade himself that the blows are given in good
earnest, as he can that they who strike them are kings
or princes." Dryden acknowledges, however, that death
is not a fit subject for stage representation; But if the
English show too much of the action, the French show
too little;

The French drama observes the "unities" more
strictly, but even Corneille acknowledges that these are
a great limitation and constraint; Dryden claims that
a strict observance of unity of place and of unbroken
scenes leads to some absurdities and to the omission of
many beauties.

In regard to c) — Here Dryden takes a middle
stand; He finds the ancients deficient in their observance
of the "unities", and yet condemns the French for too
strictly binding themselves by rules, which, as these,
tend to constrain the author and make the plot too
barren; on the other hand, he praises Ben Jonson's
"The Silent Woman" for its perfect regularity.* Both
Shakespeare and Fletcher have written "some plays
which are almost exactly formed" — "Ben Jonson's are
for the most part regular", Dryden adds — and in their
"irregular plays, there is a more masculine fancy and
greater spirit in the writing than there is in any of
the French."

In regard to d) — Dryden repeats, practically,
what he has already advanced in the Dedication to
"The Rival Ladies": Comedy is left out of the question
altogether, and rhyme is defended, for *serious plays*, on
the following grounds: —

---

* This drama *("Epicoene, or The Silent Woman")* appeared
in 1609.

Rhyme may be made, by the proper placing of words, as natural in a play as blank verse, and is, after all, in itself as natural, for in ordinary conversation one does not use either; the former has besides the advantage of sweetness of sound;

As a serious play represents nature wrought up to a much higher pitch than in ordinary life, so is it perfectly proper to represent the character as speaking in heroic rhyme, which is more exalted than ordinary prose. If blank verse be not suitable for an ordinary occasional poem (as has been acknowledged* how can it be proper for the drama, which (according to Aristotle) occupies a place above even the epic?

Rhyme in repartee is no more unnatural than blank verse, inasmuch as either must appear as the result of confederation and consultation between the actors. There is a "quick and poignant brevity" in repartee, and when this is "joined with the cadency and sweetness of rhyme" the "last perfection" is added;

The majesty of verse does not suffer through clothing ordinary conversation (such as giving commands to a servant) in rhyme, for a good poet will, by a tasteful arrangement and choice of words, avoid any vulgarity in this respect. Besides, such conversation would be no less little and mean if clothed in blank verse.

Dryden takes up again and defends against the attack of "Crites", one particular argument advanced in favor of rhyme in the Dedication to "The Rival Ladies" — namely, that it circumscribes a too luxuriant imagination. As "the second thoughts are usually the best, as receiving the maturest digestion from judgment, and the last and most mature product of those thoughts being artful and labored verse, it may well be inferred that verse is a great help to a luxuriant fancy."

---

* Namely, by "Crites"; in his attack upon rhyme.

III.

A Defence of an Essay of Dramatic Poesy, published
in 1668.*

In 1668, shortly after the publication of Dryden's
"Essay of Dramatic Poesy", appeared the tragedy "The
Great Favorite or The Duke of Lerma" by Sir Robert
Howard, Dryden's brother-in-law and the Crites of the
Essay. In this many exceptions are taken to the argu-
ments advanced in the Essay, particularly on the sub-
jects of rhyme and the unities. Dryden retorted in the
"Defence of an Essay of Dramatic Poesy", which was
prefixed to the second edition of "The Indian Emperor",**
Though clever, witty and even stinging in its replies
to the lumbering attacks of Sir Robert Howard, this
"Defence" brings but little that is new in helping us
to determine Dryden's individual critical opinions on the
two points mentioned. Dryden says, in effect;

The naturalness or unnaturalness of rhyme cannot
be demonstrated; "if it cause delight it is sufficient,
for delight is the chief end of poesie";

A "bare imitation" will not serve the ends of a
serious play, for the poet must use "all the arts and
ornaments of poesie" to heighten the converse he is to
imitate; which converse should be "such as, strictly
considered, could never be supposed spoken by any
without premeditation". A play will not be thought
to be the result of the confederation of several persons
who have the faculty of speaking in verse, *extempore*;
but is supposed to be the work of the poet, imitating
or representing the conversation of several persons;

One great objection to prose, is that it is too much
like nature and the use of it would be so near an imitation as to destroy the artistic quality of the work;

---

* Arnold's Edition of the Essay, p. 100 seq.
** The "Defence" is not to be found in all copies of this
second edition and was afterwards suppressed, never appearing
again in print during Dryden's life-time. Compare "Edition"
Vol. I p. 86 and Vol. II p. 290; also Arnold, p. 100.

Rhyme seems, by common consent of modern poets, to be the natural successor of ancient verse; which shows that the former "obtained the end — which was to please", and Dryden acknowledges that he is ruled by the desire to delight the age in which he lives. He concludes the defence of verse, however, by saying that it is, "after all, a very indifferent thing", to him, "whether it obtain or not" — which utterance is a most convenient, and for Dryden quite characteristic, way of precluding further arguments against his then preference for verse.

In answering his critic in that masterful style which makes this "Defence" a worthy appendix to the "Essay", Dryden claims that the only foundation of dramatic poetry, since and for all times, is the „imitation of nature"; and refers to the definition of a play which had been settled upon by the four disputants in the Essay; namely, that a play ought to be: "A just and lively image of human nature, representing its passions and humours, and the changes of fortune to which it is subject, for the delight and instruction of mankind." The means to be used in attaining this end are such as were employed by the dramatists of both ancient and modern times, and Dryden calls upon the "authority of Aristotle and Horace" and the "rules and examples of Ben Jonson and Corneille" to support the statements made in the Essay regarding these "means"; by which we are to understand (in this "Defence", at least) practically only a proper employment of the unities of time and place. In reply to Sir Robert Howard's somewhat illogical attacks upon Dryden's utterances in the Essay as regards these unities, they are again discussed, and we find Dryden willing to allow a certain latitude in regard to *place* — the scene of action may be laid in "several places in the same town or city, or places adjacent to each other in the same country" — but he contends that "nearer and fewer those imaginary places are, the greater resemblance they will have to truth". His conclusions regarding the unity of *time* are: "That the imaginary time of every play ought to be contrived into as narrow a compass as the nature of the plot, the quality of the persons, and variety of accidents will allow". In comedy, he would not exceed twenty-four or thirty hours; to tragedy he allows a larger space, following in these views the practise of Ben Jonson.

IV.

The Preface to "An Evening's Love, or The Mock Astrologer"; published in 1668 (Edition, Vol. III; p. 227, seq.).

The subject of this preface is the nature of comedy and the distinction between it and farce; and though containing but few direct statements of opinion upon dramatic technique, it is of considerable importance in judging of Dryden's position towards comedy in general. He regards comedy as "in its own nature, inferior to all sorts of dramatic writing", but yet it is nobler than farce.

Jonson, and Dryden's contemporaries make an error in representing in comedy the "follies of particular persons".

Dryden approves most "the mixed way of comedy; that which is neither all wit nor all humor, but the result of both".

The characters in comedy must be „well chosen, and kept distant from interfering with each other"; which is not the case with Shakespeare and Fletcher.

Comedy must contain more of the "ornaments of wit"; which he gives (after Quintilian) as being the *urbana, venusta, salsa, faceta* and others, which are wanting in Ben Jonson.

Repartee is "the greatest grace of comedy", and yet even here the author must be careful to avoid "the superfluity and waste of wit" of Dryden's pre-decessors, particularly Shakespeare and Fletcher. The wit of the repartee must be suited to the person uttering it; "A witty coward, and a witty brave, must speak differently."

In defending himself against the charge of violating "the law of comedy, which is to reward virtue, and punish vice", by making "debauched persons" the heroes of the drama to which this essay forms a preface, Dryden denies that such a law has "been constantly observed in comedy, either by the ancient or modern poets". It is necessary here to distinguish between the rules of tragedy and comedy; In tragedy, "the laws of justice are more strictly observed" and vice is punished for the sake of example. In comedy, "the chief end is divertisement and delight", the persons represented, too, "are of a lower quality", the vices and faults such as are common to all mankind and which excite "pity and commiseration; not detestation and horror"; therefore „comedy is not so much obliged to the punishment of faults which it represents, as tragedy".

V.

The Preface to "Tyrannic Love, or The Royal Martyr"; published in 1670 (Edition, Vol. III; p. 369, seq.).

The plot of the play is the martyrdom of St. Catherine, and in this preface Dryden defends the dramatic representation of religious subjects, as follows:

Dryden maintains, "against the enemies of the stage, that patterns of piety, decently represented, and equally removed from the extremes of superstition and profaness, may be of excellent use to second the precepts of our religion";

"The harmony of words", like the solemn music in churches, "elevates the soul to a sense of devotion"; and, added to this, comes the action: so that the soul is charmed by "what it sees and hears", and seized "with a secret veneration of things celestial".

He is not to be charged with profaness or irreligion on account of the part of Maximin in this play, for when this "bloody tyrant" and "persecutor of the church" is represented as speaking against religion this is only in keeping with historical tradition and with nature. It is not improper to present "a person of such principles" and a scoffer at religion upon the stage, for the Holy Scriptures contain records of the lives and sayings of many "wicked and profane persons", and Dryden makes no other use of the character of Maximin than as in the Holy Scriptures — to set him as "a sea-mark for those who behold to avoid": Besides, the requirements of dramatic art are fulfilled, for the punishment of Maximin's crime follows immediately upon its execution.

Dryden's position as regards the heroic drama is marked by the statement; "Heroic representations are not limited but with the extremest bounds of what is credible".

--

VI.

The Essay *"Of Heroic Plays"*, prefixed to *"The Conquest of Granada"*; first published in 1672. (Edition Vol. IV, p. 18, seq.)

At the beginning the subject of heroic verse is again mentioned, and some of the arguments in its favor repeated; although Dryden concedes that it may be left free to every man to write in verse or not, according to his talent, or the taste of his audience. Turning then to the subject proper, Dryden makes the celebrated statement; "An heroic play ought to be an imitation, in little, of an heroic poem"; its subject should, consequently, be "love and valour".

He defends the supernatural element in heroic poetry — the poet must be allowed this free scope of imagination: "The greatest part of mankind" have believed in magic and in apparitions; and poets are, in all cases

better able (through the aid of fancy) to deal with such
dark and doubtful questions. Nor is the employment
of spectres and magic in heroic poetry unnatural; for
such things may exist, and "whatever is, or may be, is
not properly unnatural." What applies to an heroic
poem applies also to an heroic play; and as the heroic
poem, from its high rank as a species of composition,
is most worthy of imitation, so the drama has the advantage of representing in action that which the poem
merely relates.

He also defends his frequent use of spectacular
effects, such as fighting and the sound of martial music:
They are necessary "to produce the effect of an heroic
play"; which is to say, that the imagination of the
audience is to be raised into believing, for the time
being, that what is beheld "on the theatre, is really
performed". The poet is to strive to a complete mastery
over the minds of his audience; "for though our fancy
will contribute to its own deceit, yet a writer ought
to help its operation."

VII.

"*Apology for Heroic Poetry and Poetic Licence*",
prefixed to "*The State of Innocence*", published in 1674.
(Edition, Vol. V, p. 111, seq.)

In this, Dryden defends certain features of the
"heroic" style; among them even the rant and bombast
(as others than Dryden would be inclined to call them)
which are so characteristic of this form of dramatic art.

"The boldest strokes of poetry, when they are
managed artfully, are those which most delight the
reader"; By these "boldest strokes" we are to understand,
chiefly, the use of metaphors and other figures of speech.
Their use is defended by the example of the ancients,
and because they have pleased generally "and through
all ages". The poet's first-duty is to copy nature, and

Dryden contends "that those things which delight all ages, must have been an imitation of nature". The figures of rhetoric were introduced on account of the effect they had upon the audience. Even catachresis and hyperbole have taken their place among the "figures", and can be, when used judiciously, of great effect; — like the lights and shades in painting, which throw the figures into bolder relief. Figures are "principally to be used in passion", since a person does not "reason rightly or talk calmly" when in a passion, and then figures are natural. But the poet must be guided by a cool discretion, which will forbid anything too extravagant in this line.

The question of the introduction of supernatural elements into heroic poetry is also discussed, but nothing new is advanced beyond the remarks upon the same subject in the "Essay on Heroic Plays": — the poet has certain liberties; the Scriptures authorize the description of immaterial substances; things above us we describe by comparing them to things we know.

As regards Poetic Licence Dryden defines it as "the liberty of speaking things in verse, which are beyond the severity of prose" and this liberty has been "from all ages" the birthright of poets; but must, however, be varied according to the language and times of each poet. "Sublime subjects ought to be adorned with the sublimest, and consequently often, with the most figurative expressions".

VIII.

Preface to "All for Love, or The World well Lost", published in 1678, (Edition. Vol. V, p. 326, seq.)

This play is an adaptation of Shakespeare's "Antony and Cleopatra", and consequently Dryden's remarks are chiefly an explanation and defence of the lines followed in his attempt to make this masterpiece agreeable to the taste of his times.

The hero of such a tragic poem "ought not to be of perfect virtue", since he then cannot with justice be made unhappy; "nor yet altogether wicked", since then he would not excite pity, so Dryden takes a middle course.

Dryden finds an error in the character of Octavia as drawn by Shakespeare, inasmuch as she absorbs some of the pity which should center in the chief characters, Antony and Cleopatra.

In defending the quarrel scene between Octavia and Cleopatra (Dryden's own invention and not found in Shakespeare) he criticizes the "nicety of manners" of the French stage, which would not have allowed such a scene. Certain actions are not fit for representation, nor should an author indulge in "broad obscenities in words"; although such a scene as the above is not to be condemned so long as "kept within the bounds of modesty". We must not allow the French to prescribe to us in such matters, until they have created something really much superior.

Dryden has endeavored "to follow the practice of the ancients" in this play; but yet he considers their models, though regular, as being "too little for English tragedy, which requires to be built in a larger compass".

He professes to imitate Shakespeare in the style of this play, and in order to do this more freely has not used rhyme, though he does not condemn his own former use of it. As a matter of fact, however, Dryden was, at this time, undergoing the process which finally ended in abandoning rhymed verse altogether.

IX.

The Essay: "The Grounds of Criticism in Tragedy"; prefixed to "Troilus and Cressida, or Truth Found too Late", which was published in 1679. (Edition, Vol. VI, p. 260, seq.)

Dryden states his endeavor in this essay to be;
"To discover the grounds and reasons of all criticism"
(with application, however, only to Tragedy) as a help
to the solution of the two questions — In how far
Shakespeare and Fletcher should be imitated in their
tragedies; and, secondly, in what ways the two named
authors differ from each other. The opening pages are
scarcely more than a variation on the theme (stated
after Aristotle) — "Tragedy is an imitation of one entire, great, and probable action, not told, but represented; which, by moving in us fear and pity, is conducive
to the purging of those two passions in our minds."

Dryden urges the necessity that the action be *one*;
as an interweaving of two independent actions tends to
distract the attention of the audience and so to destroy
the purpose of the author. He leaves himself a convenient exit for escape, however, by stating that, "to
give us the pleasure of variety", the combination of a
principal and a subservient action „has obtained on the
English stage."

Regarding the other points of the above dictum
Dryden brings nothing new, but simply comments at
considerable length upon them and brings Rapin and
Bossu to his support. But these French critics derive
all their authority from Aristotle. The chief importance
to us of the pages which Dryden devotes to this consideration is that they show that he (at the time of
writing at least) was entirely in favor of the "regular"
style of writing, except in the case of the unity of action,
where (as we have just seen) he seems willing to allow a
certain latitude.

Hereupon Dryden answers the first question, stated
at the beginning, as follows; "that we ought to follow
Shakespeare and Fletcher in their plots, so far only as
they have copied the excellencies of those who invented
and brought to perfection dramatic poetry." He allows
exceptions in favor of the alterations which "religion,
custom of countries, idioms of language, etc.", have made

"in the superstructures, but not in the foundation of the design."*

Dryden then considers the *"manners"* of a tragedy, which he defines as meaning — „those inclinations, whether natural or acquired, which move and carry us to actions, good, bad, or indifferent, or which incline the persons to such actions." The proper treatment of manners can be comprised under four general heads:

First, "they must be apparent;" in other words, the persons must be characterized by some manners peculiar to each which must appear in their "actions and discourse:"

Secondly, they "must be suitable," or adapted to the age, sex, dignity, etc. of the personages represented:

Thirdly, they must have resemblance to the persons to whom they are ascribed; by which is meant that when a poet is describing an historical character he is bound to represent him "not contrary to that which fame has reported him to have been;" and Fourthly, they must be „constant and equal, that is, maintained the same through the whole design."

From the manners are derived the *characters*, for these are only "the inclinations, as they appear in the several persons of the poem;" since character is "that which distinguishes one man from another." A character must not be "one particular virtue, or vice, or passion only," but a composition of qualities which are not opposed to one another in the same person. As already stated, the hero of the tragedy (in order that he may have the sympathies of audience) ought to be distinguished by virtue rather than by vice; and the concernment (i. e. the pity and terror) of the spectators must be enlisted allmost entirely for this one character. "Terror and compassion work but weakly when they are divided into many persons."

Dryden treats also the *"passions"* under the general head of manners; meaning — "anger, hatred,

---

* Dryden's answer to the second question (on the difference between Shakespeare and Fletcher) I purposely omit, since it does not bear upon the present investigation.

love, ambition, jealousy, revenge, etc., as they are shown in this or that person of the play." The quality of describing these naturally must be born with the poet, but this gift must be aided by acquired knowledge, or the author will fall into many errors, which "proceed from want of judgment in the poet, and from being unskilled in the principles of moral philosophy." The poet must restrain and carefully "manage his strength": The "roar of passion" will captivate only the vulgar; and if all the characters rant, there can be no distinguishing of one from another. The poet "who would concern an audience by describing of a passion" must prepare it first, "and not rush upon it all at once." There must be nothing in the discourse to prevent the "moving of the passions." Therefore are to be avoided; "too many accidents," and unseasonable wit and sententiousness — "no man is at leisure to make sentences and similes, when his soul is in an agony."

The fourth property of manners is not touched upon, and the essay concludes rather abruptly with a quotation from the French critic Rapin, which defends the necessity for rules in poetic composition.

Although properly falling outside of the purpose of this paper, I cannot leave the above Essay without noticing one or two points which must surely force themselves upon the attention of every careful reader of Dryden's critical writings. Although, in my mind, even superior to the "Essay of Dramatic Poesy" as a piece of easy, masterful prose, it has certain defects which detract from its value as an attempt to determine the necessary qualities of serious dramatic composition. One may note, for instance, that Dryden's statements (as he himself acknowledges) are based, for the greater part, not upon individual investigation and observation, but upon "Aristotle with his interpreters, and Horace and Longinus;" as also, it may be added, upon such comparatively unimportant critics as Rapin and Bossu. There is also a tendency to enlarge upon some points at great length (such as the treatment of the "passions") with considerable show of acquaintance with

classical authors; and to pass over others (such as the
constancy and equality of the "manners") with fewer
words than the subject demands. The most disagreeable
feature of all is Dryden's evident desire to defend himself, both for his former offences in dramatic authorship
and for his present way of thinking now that his eyes
are opened to the way "the ancients" (who have harass-
ed him and led him into more than one inconsistency
from the very beginning of his theoretical utterances)
thought and acted upon certain points. And the abrupt
close, which is explained by a desire to "first see how
this will relish with the age" before he proceeds "to the
thoughts and expressions suitable to a tragedy" (which
plan was never carried out, so far as we know) makes
the impression that Dryden found his subject becoming
too much of a burden for him and took this convenient
way of ending his considerations.

The „Grounds of Criticism in Tragedy" is Dryden's
last important theoretical essay, but his occasional critical remarks upon dramatic art ceased only with his
dramatic activity. Tor the sake of completeness I add
therefore the following:

X.

*The Dedication to "The Spanish Friar, or The
Double Discovery;"* published in 1681, (Edition, Vol. VI,
p. 402, seq.)

Dryden intimates here his resolution to abandon
bombast, and repeats some observations upon this subject already made in "The Grounds of Criticism in Tragedy:"
"Nothing is truly sublime that is not just and proper."
In such passages where dramatic poetry rises to a higher
expression of emotion, "the strength and vehemence of
figures should be suited to the occasion, the subject and
the persons."

In this play Dryden has broken the rule that the

action should be *one*, and has composed a double plot — "for the pleasure of variety" The audiences have (he states) grown weary of continued melancholy scenes; tragedies, with the exception of those written in verse, must (in order to succeed) be "lightened with a course of mirth".

XI.

Preface to "Albion and Albanius"; published in 1685. (Edition, Vol. VII, p. 228, seq.)

This production was named by Dryden "an Opera"; although, as Saintsbury remarks *, the name of "Masque" would be the most proper classification. Accordingly, this preface is principally a definition and characterization of the operatic form of drama, which Dryden defines as; "A poetical tale, or fiction, represented by vocal and instrumental music, adorned with scenes, machines, and dancing." The personages are gods, goddesses and heroes; that is, in general, supernatural beings. The characters being supernatural and the subject "extended beyond the limits of human nature", many things may be allowed which would not be allowable in other styles of dramatic composition; as, for instance, the introduction of incidents which would otherwise seem impossible. Yet propriety is to be observed even here, so that the author shall cause each god to do only that which properly belongs (according to mythology) to his particular province. As the personages sing, instead of speak, so the "lofty, figurative and majestical expressions" which would otherwise be fitting for such characters, can be less frequently used. The part which is sung "must abound in the softness and variety of numbers; its principal intention being to please hearing rather than to gratify the understanding. Lest it should appear preposterous "that rhyme,

---

* Edition, loc. cit., p. 227.

on any consideration should take place of reason", Dryden lays down a fundamental proposition which we meet with in other essays of his and which is characteristic of one side of his criticism, namely; "The first inventors of any art or science, provided they have brought it to perfection, are, in reason, to give laws to it; and according to their model, all after-undertakers are to build". So must the writer of operas imitate the Italians. He then allows that sometimes persons of meaner origin than "gods, goddesses and heroes" may be introduced; particularly when the time of the opera is that Golden Age when mortals and deities were on more familiar terms of intercourse. He mentions sheperds as being particularly fitted for admission among the Dramatis Personae, since their calling was the "most innocent and the most happy" and because they had the most leisure for verse-making and love; which latter quality is absolutely essential to an Opera. It is worth mentioning, *en passant*, how Dryden comes to make this exception to his dictum; He considers, namely, the origin and history of the opera in Italy and it occurs to him that one of the first and best known examples of the class in that country is a *pastoral* opera — the "Pastor Fido" of Guarini. So Dryden, whose whole critical apparatus was very largely dependent upon tradition and the opinions of other critics, immediately opens up his definition again and lets in the shepherds.

XII.

The Preface to "Don Sebastion"; published in 1690. (Edition, Vol. VII, d. 306, seq.)

It is worthy of notice that in the opening words of this preface Dryden expresses the feeling that writing for the theatre is a "hard necessity", which only his "bad circumstances" force him to continue. It is also somewhat surprising to read the statement that "love and honour (the mistaken topics of tragedy) are quite worn out" — certainly a great concession for one to make who depended so largely upon these two elements in his heroic plays; who considered them, in fact, the very bones and sinews of such dramas!

In defence of his treatment of the plot of this play, Dryden lays down the law, that: "Where the event of a play is left doubtful, there the poet is left master. He may raise what he pleases on that foundation, provided he makes it of a piece, and according to the rules of probability". An author is not be accused of plagiarism when he works over incidents or stories which have been treated before. This has been done often by both ancient and modern poets; and, besides, "the contrivance, the new turn, and new characters alter the property" and make it that of the author who last writes.

He has not followed strictly "the three mechanic rules of unity", since "the genius of the English cannot bear too regular a play". Dryden excuses himself for his "irregularitees" (as he would once have called them) on the ground that "to gain a greater beauty, it is lawful for a poet to supersede a less".

The remaining critical utterances of Dryden which bear upon my purpose may be grouped together under the following section:

XIII.

a) In the *Dedication to "King Arthur, a Dramatic Opera"*, published in 1691, (Edition, Vol. VIII, p. 129 seq.) we find, practically, only a repetition of the statements made in the Preface to "Albion and Albanius."

b) *"Cleomenes, or The Spartan Hero"*; published in 1692 (Edition, Vol. VIII, p. 203, seq.) is a tragedy without a comic underplot. Dryden acknowledges in the *Preface* (loc. cit. p. 219, seq.) that this is "the natural and true way", but yet it was a "bold attempt" on his part, since such single plots are "not to the genius of the nation". He introduces a noisy mob in one scene, in order (as he says) "to gratify the barbarous part of the audience". Such scenes are, however, as he considers, degrading to a tragedy when represented. The neglect of the unity of time is excused on the ground that he wished to introduce a particular scene; and, "in such a case, it is better to trespass on a rule than leave out a beauty."

c) *The Dedication* to Dryden's last play, "*Love Triumphant, or Nature will Prevail*", published in 1694 (Edition, Vol. VIII, p. 371 seq.) is almost entirely only a defence of this play, but is so characteristic of Dryden's attitude toward dramatic criticism that a short *résumé* is not without value. The catastrophe is brought about by "a change of will", which Aristotle has declared not to be of "the first order of beauty"; but Dryden draws himself out of this difficulty by asserting that the laws of dramatic writing (as set forth by that philosopher) were drawn "from the authorities and examples of the Greek poets", who so suffered from "poverty of invention" that they were often forced to make the chief person change his mind without "art or preparation". In other words, that this change was handled so clumsily was the reason for its condemnation by Aristotle; who would (thinks Dryden) have judged differently could he have seen such a play as the "Cinna" of Corneille.

One of the principal characters in this play, Alphonso, has his true parentage discovered in the *third* act, which might be considered an innovation (though Dryden claims that dramatic art should be allowed to make changes for the better) were not a precedent for such a course to be found in Menander and Terence.*

---

* Dryden acknowledges that he "casually discovered this precedent afterwards", which is very characteristic for his dramaturgy! Worthy of notice is also the fact that in the case of the "change of will" he overthrows the authority of the Ancients; whereas, in the case of an important piece of dramatic business occuring in the third act, he is visibly relieved to find an athority in classical literature.

In this play, as in several others, Dryden has not
adhered slavishly to the unity of place, as prescribed
by the Ancients, though the scene remains in the same
city. Those who object to allowing a poet such a
liberty call it very ridiculous "for an audience to suppose
themselves some times to be in a field, sometimes in a
garden, and at other times in a chamber", and it is
true that a frequent change of scene is more absurd
than a strict observance of the unity of place; but as
a matter of fact "it is an original absurdity for the
audience to suppose themselves to be in any other place
than in the very theatre in which they sit".

The "double action", each of which is of a "different
species", cannot be defended by the example of the
Ancients; for, though they employed double actions,
these "were of the same species": But Dryden considers
it defence enough to say that he has written according
to the genius of the English nation, which loves variety;
though he calls this love a "publice vice", and would
be pleased to write differently, were the audience cured
of it.

The above pages strive to give, in abstract, that
which we seem justified in considering as Dryden's
individual opinions on dramatic art. That this is, after
all, but one feature of the essays, prefaces and dedications
which I have analysed, scarce needs to be stated; in
many cases that which was needed for the purpose of
this paper had to be dug out of a heap of fulsome
flattery addressed to some lord or other man of influence,
or sifted out from among the chaff of a mass of irrele-
vant matter: Nor does the chief value of these productions consist in their relation to the above mentioned
theme; for on the one side their masterful, often fas-
cinating, style, and on the other the light thrown by
them on the condition of English literature at Dryden's
time, still can attract readers for whom the dramas
of Dryden have with few exceptions, little interest.

The abstracts which I have given above prove, as
I hope, the marked personal and subjective character

of Dryden's dramatic criticism, which is besides, in nearly every case of an occasional nature, i. e. having reference to some particular play of his own—almost without exception to that one to which it is prefixed or appended in an essay, preface or dedication: Even when Dryden speaks of the "present age" or the "genius of English" we feel that he means himself and his own writings. Hereby we must not forget how thoroughly Dryden was subservient to the royal and popular tastes, which were, in his day, nearly identical, owing to the influence exerted by the court upon all classes of society. So although he may, at times, have wished to stand above the debasement and corruption of his age, yet from motives of policy, he chose to swim with the muddy current. A man who will change his religions and political belief as often and as easily as did Dryden, can hardly be expected to courageously maintain a higher standard than the taste of that corrupt court and public upon whom he depended for applause and subsistence. That he could have done better and nobler things than he has left us, is made evident to any reader of even his worst literary work (his plays) by the many flashes of a higher genius which break in upon one in the midst of bombast or coarseness; and also that he would have done this had he but possessed the moral courage, is proved by many utterances in which he speaks of himself as the "slave of the public", the "Sisyphus of the stage", etc., which show that he was conscious of his pandering to a base taste and regretted it.

The personal, subjective and occasional character of Dryden's theorizings prevent him from being regarded as an authority on the drama in general. Who would, for instance, at the present time, put Jonson or Fletcher above Shakespeare as a dramatist in the confident manner of Dryden? Even the celebrated passage in the "Essay of Dramatic Poesy" which gives to Shakespeare "the largest and most comprehensive soul" scarce atones for such a one sided judgment. We might have expected from so great a poet an estimate of Shakespeare which would have restored him, in that day of prevailing French taste, to his proper place; but this would have been flying in the face of court and populace, for it is scarcely to be gainsayed that Dryden, here as elsewhere, trimmed his sails according to the prevailing wind. Therefore in testing the theories and rules of the *critic* Dryden, we must consider only the *playwright* Dryden, who made the rules to suit himself and abandoned them when it pleased him. I have devoted so much space above to the analyses of Dryden's theoretical and critical essays on account of the examination, which here follows, of the relations between Dryden's theory and praxis in dramatic composition.

PART SECOND

DRYDEN'S DRAMATIC PRAXIS AND ITS RELATION TO HIS THEORY.

One important fact must be kept continually in mind in an attempt to apply Dryden's theory to his own dramatic productions, namely; that the essays, etc., which I have above summarized, were in each case written *after* the drama to which they are attached. Even the "Essay of Dramatic Poesy", which might appear to be an independent production, was written in 1665, after the representation of "The Wild Gallant" and "The Rival Ladies", and after Dryden had assisted Sir Robert Howard in the composition of "The Indian Queen" which was acted in 1664. His own „Indian Emperor" had also been written and acted before the compsition of "The Essay of Dramatic Poesy"; which latter might, indeed, find its proper place in his Works just before the "Defense of the Essay", as a preface to this drama. This fact confirms also what I have hinted at above and which has been pointed out by several who have written on Dryden *, namely; that his criticism is in every instance determined by the particular occasion when it was written, and undergoes some important changes in the course of his dramatic activity. In view of this, it is necessary, in order to

---

* For instance Riedel; in a Rostock dissertation of 1868: "Dryden's Influence on the Dramatic Literature of England", pp. 27, 28 — "His criticism is in every instance occasional", etc.

properly apply his theories and criticisms to his own writings, to subject each play separately to an examination with regard to the ideas which Dryden held at the time of its composition; or, to speak more properly, which he may have convinced himself that he held in order to suit them to that particular purpose. With Comedy we have but little to do, since Dryden's utterances on this head are few; nor are his comedies many in number, or, with one or two exceptions, of particular dramatic worth. He expresses his distaste for this style of writing and his conviction of his unfitness for it in more than one passage of his theoretical writings. Our attention is therefore to be chiefly directed to his tragedies, and yet the first play which we have to consider (though only cursorily) which is at the same time Dryden's first dramatic composition, is a comedy, namely:

I.

"The Wild Gallant": (Ed., Vol. II, p. 21, seq.) first acted in 1663, but not printed until 1669, after it had been revised and re-acted. The short preface which accompanied the publication, gives no expresed theory of Dryden's upon which to base a consideration of his practice in its composition, and on that account was omitted in the first part of this paper. Dryden's first definite utterances on the nature of Comedy are contained in the preface to 'An Evening's Love", which did not appear until 1671. In the preface to "The Wild Gallant" he simply states the opinion that Comedy is the "most difficult part" of dramatic poetry and acknowledges that it was a bold attempt for him to begin with this style of dramatic work; also that the play is "uncorrect". In the Epilogue to the revised version he also states that:

"Of all dramatic writing, comic wit,
    As 'tis the best, so 'tis most hard to hit",

since characters and incidents must be described which are familiar to all, and in regard to which each person is justified in criticizing the author's performance of his task. Judging the play by the above remarks of Dryden we find that he has, in one respect, followed that which he hints at as a standard of Comedy; for though he acknowledges a foreign (presumably French or Spanish) original, the scene is laid in London in his own time, and the characters are such as every one of his audience must have often seen, and could recognize readily as having been drawn from the social life of that day. As to the "hitting" of the "comic wit" one would think that Dryden's audiences must have been well pleased; for the play is quite as broad, though by no means deficient in genuine humor, as any of the Restoration comedies. For a further characterization of "The Wild Gallant", I refer to Saintsbury's remarks in the Edition; loc. cit., pp. 24 and 25. It is written throughout in prose.

II.

"*The Rival-Ladies*", a Tragi-Comedy, the next play of Dryden's in chronological order (Ed., Vol. II, p. 125, seq.) is preceded by the dedication noticed above.* This play contains Dryden's first attempts in the use of rhymed couplets, though a large part is written in blank verse and a portion of Scene I, Act V, in prose. Evidently Dryden was not yet so thorougly convinced of the superiority of the kind of writing defended in the Dedication as to then venture upon writing an entire drama in that form; Perhaps, too, he doubted its entire acceptability with the audience at that time. Inded, he hints at this in the words of the Dedication.— "I fear lest I shall be accused for following the new way, I mean of writing scenes in verse"; with which compare his intimation in the "Essay of Dramatic Poesy" that the

* Part First, § I.

audiences were too much prepossessed in favor of plays in blank verse* to readily accept rhyme.

The entire drama contains but 178 rhymed lines; among them six, which notwithstanding faulty rhyming (here, fear, where; and fear, there, air) are no doubt intended for triplets, and eight lines in strophe form according to the scheme; a, b, a, b, c, d, c, d. The first act contains, outside of the couplet ending the act,** but 26 lines which are rhymed and with the exception of the two triplets, in the so-called "heroic couplet". It is worthy of mention that in this short passage there are three lines which do not rhyme — a usage which Dryden advocates, for the sake of variety, in the Essay of Dramatic Poesy.*** The second Act contains only 12 rhymed lines, and these are at the end of the act. I have not included in the 178 lines in rhyme, a masque which occurs in the third Act, since such intermezzi were always in rhymed verse, so that to this act there fall only 18 lines in "heroic verse", which includes two couplets at the end of the act. The largest number are in the fourth Act, namely 108. The six couplets which occur in Act V seem, with the exception of those which terminate scenes and the act itself, of an accidental nature. From this sparing use of "the new way" it is easy to conclude that Dryden wished first to make an attempt with the taste of his audiences; perhaps, also, he was trying his own strength and fitness for this style of composition.

Notwithstanding its title of "Tragi-Comedy" there

---

* Arnold, loc. cit:—Crites says, p. 79: "I might satisfy myself to tell you, how much in vain it is for you to strive against the stream of the people's inclination". Neander replies, p. 90: "As for what you have added—that the people are not generally inclined to like this way, if it were true, it would be no wonder that betwixt the shaking off an old habit, and the introducing a new, there should be difficulty."

** It is a well known fact that these rhymed couplets at the end of a scene or an act are to be found in plays which otherwise are written in blank verse throughout. vide Abbott, A Shakespearian Grammar, § 515.

*** Arnold, Ed., p. 85, line 29, seq.

is but little of a tragic element in The Rival-Ladies, nor can it fall under Dryden's idea of a "serious" play, since neither the "argument" nor the "characters and persons" are "great and noble". Therefore, in turning our attention to the relation between theory and practice in this play, we cannot judge it by the principles laid down for the use of rhyme in the "Essay of Dramatic Poesy", since these (by agreement of the disputants) apply only to rhyme in tragedy.* Using what Dryden says in the Dedication** we arrive at the following results;

As regards "the only inconvenience with which rhyme can be charged", i. e. ending the lines with verbs (d); we find Dryden often enough "forced upon this rock". On this account, too, the rhymed lines do not give the effect of naturalness (e); since, in many instances, the words are placed "for rhyme sake, so unnaturally as no man would in ordinary speaking", nor is the ordering altogether so judicious (f.) that the verses make the effect of "the negligence of prose." But it is perhaps hardly possible to insist upon too exact an application of the above rules, since the number of rhymed lines in the play is so small. It may be added, however, that one feature which Dryden mentions in the Dedication (Works, l. c., p. 137) as an essential introduced by Waller;*** namely, that each couplet should contain a complete thought, is pretty closely followed in this drama.

The one passage of repartee (h) in the first Scene of the fourth Act gains, without doubt, a "particular grace" from the use of rhyme, which well sets off "the sudden smartness of the answer". This passage is the first of those scenes of quick and ready, though often far-fetched, repartee which afterwards occur so frequently between Dryden's lovers. This scene is not, however, one "of argumentation or discourse on the result of which the

---

* Arnold, loc, cit., p. 84, line 8.
** vide Part First, § 1, above; to which the following divisions refer.
*** "He (Waller) first showed us to conclude the sense, most commonly in distichs."

doing or not doing some considerable action depends":
in fact this remark of Dryden's must be understood as
applying to serious plays.

If "The Rival - Ladies" offers but little opportunity
for testing and applying his theories, the next play in
Dryden's works affords still less. I allude to:

lfl.

„*The Indian Queen*, a Tragedy;" published early in
1665. (Ed., Vol. II, p. 223, seq.)

This play is only in part of Dryden's authorship,
since it is really the work of his brother - in - law, Sir
Robert Howard. Scott, and following him, Saintsbury
(Ed., l. c., pp. 225. 226) seem certain that the incantation
scene of Act III is nearly, if not quite all Dryden's. But
an exact determination of how much falls to the lot of
each author is yet to be undertaken, is perhaps an im-
possibility. In view of these facts, I will omit any
further consideration of this play and turn to the next
in order, namely:

IV.

"*The Indian Emperor; or the Conquest of Mexico by
the Spaniards*"; first published in 1667; second edition,
with "A Defence of an Essay of Dramatic Poesy," 1668.
(Ed., Vol. II, p. 283, seq.)

This is Dryden's first great drama in the "heroic"
style. It is intended as a sequel to "The Indian Queen"
as the title-page expressly states, but Dryden is the sole
author. It is written throughout in rhymed couplets, of
which, by this time, Dryden was fully master; he felt
sure, besides, of carrying the taste of the larger part
of his audiences with him in this respect, since rhymed
plays had now become a matter of fashion.

In the application of Dryden's theories to this drama,
the Dedication to "The Rival - Ladies" may be omitted,
since it touches only upon the question of rhyme and
contains practically nothing more than is to be found

on this subject in "The Essay of Dramatic Poesy". Upon this latter and its companion-piece—"A Defence of the Essay"—and the principles therein set forth, the following consideration is based.

First, as regards the rhyme; Here we must confine ourselves to the remarks made in the "Essay" alone, since those contained in the "Defence" are of too abstract a character (dealing, as they do, with the naturalness or unnaturalness of rhyme as opposed to prose or blank verse) for the present purpose. Again, as the whole drama is rhymed, no concrete statement can be made as to the use of this form in "repartee" or in "scenes of argumentation and discourse", save that it cannot be denied that such passages (particularly the former) do seem, to our ears, better suited to this style of writing than those of either mere description or of high tragic interest.

The lines are less frequently closed with verbs, in proportion to the length of the play, than in "The Rival-Ladies", as indeed the verse throughout is more finished. In Act I, Scene II, are 24 verses in which two rhymes alternate with each other (as in one short passage in „The Rival-Ladies") after the scheme: a, b, a, b, c, d, c, d, etc. It is a remarkable fact that nowhere, in any of his theoretical or critical writings on the drama, does Dryden expressly mention this exception from the rhymed couplets which he considered as so appropriate to heroic plays.

Another point regarding this drama, for which we can refer to the "Essay" and its "Defence", is the question of the observance of the unities of Time and Place*. In both essays Dryden is careful not to commit himself to very exact statements, but allows a great deal more latitude in the treatment of both time and place than the French classical drama. The events of this play might be easily imagined as happening within six or seven days. The exact duration of the action is not easy to

---

* vide Part First, § II d); and § III, conclusion.

determine from the drama itself, although an examination
with this end in view shows that at least three days
are required. Even the time of six or seven days may
seem rather too short for Cortez to declare war against
Montezuma; to fall in love with the latter's daughter;
to gain possession of Mexico, but lose his mistress through
the jealousy of a princess who also loves him, etc.; but
those acquainted with the nature of heroic tragedy will
know how many events are often compressed into a
comparatively short space of time.* Still it is not to
be denied that Dryden has here committed one of the
errors of which he speaks in the "Defence"; namely, the
"oversight" of compressing "the accidents of a play into
a narrower compass than that in which they could naturally be produced", though this is an error which Dryden
considers pardonable, since it produces variety. The
unity of *place* does not come away much better, if it
were to be judged by the rules of the ancient and French
classic drama. Dryden has, however, objected to such
rigidity which would confine the action to but one place
throughout the whole play, and has allowed that the
scene may be laid in "several places in the same town
or city, or places adjacent to each other in the same
country". The latter clause applies to "The Indian
Emperor", the action of which takes place, throughout,
in or around the city of Mexico, with the exception of
the first Scene of the first Act which is some leagues
distant from that city. The scene changes sixteen times,
but notwithstanding the number of the changes, they are
not so great (with one exception) but that we can easily
suppose the characters of the drama to move from one
locality to another within the time of the representation.
This one exception occurs in the first Act: Scene I is
"A pleasant Indian country" at some considerable distance
from the city. Scene II is "A Temple"—
"Far from noise, without the city gate"; hither

---

* vide Holzhausen's treatise on *"Dryden's heroisches Drama"*,
in Kölbing's Englische Studien, Vols XIII, XV, XVI, which practically exhausts the subject of the heroic drama and all its characteristics.

comes "hastily" Guyomar, and reports to his father
Montezuma that he has seen the ships of the Spaniards,
and in about a hundred lines more the ceremonies in
the temple are interrupted by the arrival of Cortez and
the others who figured in the first scene! The actual
distance between the two localities, and the actual time
required to go from one to the other are certainly greater
than even the latitude which Dryden would allow without over stepping the bounds of probability*. Act IV
contains nearly as many changes of scene as can be found
in any of the older dramatists, and each scene contains
different characters from that just preceding it, as also
each new place is at a greater or less distance from the
former locality. Indeed, this act is like a series of distinct
pictures, and the time between each might well be supposed
much greater than even Dryden would have allowed,
with all his latitude.

Regarding certain remarks under *b* of the Essay we
find; First, that there are certainly a sufficient number
of "under-plots or by-concernments" to produce that
variety which Dryden considered as arising from this
practice. Without doubt these all bear a relation to
the principal plot; namely, the conquest of Mexico by
the Spaniards. That the main plot and all the side
designs hinge upon the two motives of love and honor
is an indispensable feature of the heroic drama**. Whether
or not this "variety" is so well managed as to give more
pleasure to the audience than one single design, is a
moot question, though contemporary records (judging from
Scott's introduction in the Works) pronounce that the
play met with great applause.

A second matter considered under *b* in the Essay
concerns the relative importance of the characters:

---

* To prevent misunderstanding, I must be allowed to state
that in my observations upon the unities, I speak from Dryden's
standpoint, which regards the slavish adherence to the unities of
time and place of the French dramas as the gauge by which
deviations and exceptions are to be judged or excused.

** vide Holzhausen's remarks on the heroic drama in general,
and this play in particular; l. c., § 2 and § 3 of Theil II.

Naturally, the chief personages can only be Montezuma and Cortez, and yet at least four * of the remaining persons are very nearly equal to these in importance. On this point, I should be inclined to decide that Dryden has committed a fault, even when judging him by his own liberal standard, since the four characters mentioned are not of sufficiently *secondary* importance, nor is their introduction well managed.

A third point concerns the "decorum of the stage" The only real battle scene (Act II, Scene II) is indicated and related, not represented. In the discussion upon this point in the "Essay", Dryden admits** that "death ought not to be represented"; and yet at the end of the play all but four of the principal characters have died on the stage, in two cases by their own hands: in Act V, Scene I, we have the pleasant spectacle in which "the two Spaniards and three Indians kill each other, Vasquez kills Odmar", and is shortly afterwards also slain. The torturing of Montezuma and an Indian High Priest, in Scene II of the same Act, is also a much greater concession to the supposed or real love of Dryden's audiences for "objects of horrour" than can easily be justified.

In concluding the remarks upon "The Indian Emperor", it must be said that it can by no means be considered to be based upon the only foundation of dramatic poetry, according to Dryden***, namely; "the imitation of nature", nor does it meet with the definition of what a play ought to be †: — "A just and lively imitation of human nature", etc. This would apply, however, to the whole class of heroic dramas ††, in which naturalness or an imitation

---

* Odmar and Guyomar (the two sons of Montezuma) and two female characters, Cydaria and Almeria.
** Arnold, loc. cit., p. 61, line 24, seq.
*** "Defence of the Essay", Arnold's Ed., p. 115, line 18 seq.
† Arnold, loc. cit., p. 17, line 20, seq.
†† Once more I must refer to Holzhausen's Essay in "Englische Studien", where the reader will find about all that can be said on the subject of the heroic drama, and well said. A part of this present paper was to have been taken up with a presentation of certain characteristics of the heroic tragedy, for which I had collected material *before* the appearance of Holzhausen's treatise. I beg, therefore, that any remarks I make upon this subject be considered the result of individual investigation.

of nature would at once destroy the entire "heroic" character. It is not the place here to discuss in how far the drama, and particularly tragedy, should or should not be an exact pattern of nature or whether such exact copying would not be inartistic because too grossly realistic: But Dryden had set up such a standard, and in this play, at least, with its absurd notions of love and honor, he has fallen short of his ideal.

Dryden's next play in chronological order is:

V.

"*Secret Love*; or *the Maiden Queen*"; published in 1668. (Edition, Vol. II, p. 413, seq.)

This is a tragi-comedy, inasmuch as it combines a serious and a comic action. This style of writing was considered by Dryden to be one of the greatest advantages of the English drama over the French* up to the death of Richelieu, since when it appeared also in French plays. A perusal of the Preface and the Prologue to this play would lead one to expect a drama as strictly written as any of Racine's; for in the first Dryden says:** "This play is regular according to the strictest of dramatic laws;" and the second contains the following lines:***

> "He who writ this, not without pains and thought,
> From French and English theatres has brought
> The exactest rules, by which a play is wrought.
>
> The unities of action, place, and time;
> The scenes unbroken, and a mingled chime
> Of Jonson's humour, with Corneille's rhyme."

---

* vide Part First, § II, *b*, of this paper: and Arnold, Ed., pp. 55, 56.
** Ed. Vol. II, p. 418.
*** Ed., Vol. II, p. 422.

But the double action proves that one of the unities has been neglected. Regarding *place;* — there are in the entire play but three or four localities (all of them within the precints of the royal court) and but six changes of scene, as the locality remains unchanged throughout an entire act, except in Act IV where it is once changed. This is certainly very nearly "regular", even more so than Dryden considered necessary in his "Defence of the Essay". The unity of *time* has been observed with the greatest exactness, since the imaginary time of the play does not exceed twelve hours (is perhaps included in one afternoon) as nearly as can be judged by internal evidence:* that this seems too "narrow a compass" for the "variety of accidents" is a criticism which applies to many other plays of the "regular" type. The assertion of the Prologue that the scenes are unbroken, is true with the exception mentioned above in the fourth act, where the scene changes from "the walks near the court" to "the Queen's apartments". "Corneille's rhyme" (i. e. the heroic couplet) does not, however, appear everywhere in the play, since by far the larger part is in a mixture of prose and blank verse; the former occuring throughout in the comic scenes. There are only four rhymed passages of any length; in each case a scene "of argumentation or discourse" or of repartee, though this cannot be made a rule for this play, since other scenes of the above description are in blank verse. Besides these longer passages each act terminates with a couplet, and some of the exits are marked in the same way. Otherwise rhyme is but sparingly used and its occurrence seems almost accidental. Taking all the above facts into consideration, the play is neither regular according to

---

* In Act II the Queen says to Philocles "See me no more this day"; in Act III he is again taken into favor after his banishment of "scarce half an hour ago". Celadon has been accepted as a lover on trial by Florimel in Act II; in Act III he mentions his "fidelity to you this long hour and a half". During that same afternoon the events of Act IV take place (cf. "the invitation to sup this afternoon", end of Act III) which are immediately followed by those of Act V.

the French standard, nor has Dryden adhered entirely to his own principles in its composition. One or two general faults of the characterization and action are either excused or acknowledged by Dryden himself in the Preface, and cannot, therefore, be considered here.

Since Dryden had, up to this time, made no remarks on the technicalities of dramatic composition in comedy, his next play can be passed over with a few words. I refer to:

VI.

"*Sir Martin Mar-all or The Feigned Innocence*"; published in 1668. (Edition, Vol. III, p. 1, seq.)
   This is practically only an adaptation by Dryden of a piece whose real author was the Duke of Newcastle, so that it would be somewhat fruitless to judge of this play as if it were an original production of Dryden's. His share in it was probably to make it effective for representation, and to add the wit and humor. Although written in prose there are occasional traces of what Saintsbury* calls "bastard blank verse". The end of each act is marked by the usual rhymed couplet. As the play is, to all intents and purposes, only a translation of Molière's "L'Etourdi" (with some additions of coarseness and wit) it is not surprising that the unities are as strictly observed as in its original; though some changes might have been expected (after Dryden's criticisms upon the French drama in the Essay) particularly in the "unbroken scenes".

● ————

VII.

"*The Tempest, or The Enchanted Island,*" first published in 1670; (Edition, Vol. III, p. 99, seq.) is perhaps even less Dryden's performance than the last-mentioned

---

* Edition, l. c., p. 39, note.

play. It is the work of Sir William Davenant, and Dryden's share of the drama was, according to Scott,[*] principally in adapting it for representation.[**] This drama, in view of the above fact, falls naturally outside the purpose of this paper; and it only remains to be said that, notwithstanding the high praise of Shakespeare expressed in the Prologue, this adaptation of his "Tempest" reflects no credit on the good taste, or veneration for the great poet, of either of the authors concerned in its composition.

VIII.

"*An Evening's Love,* or *The Mock Astrologer*"; published in 1668. (Edition, Vol. III, p. 227, seq.)

This is the first comedy of Dryden's which can be judged by distinct utterances of his upon the nature and technique of this style of dramatic composition; Such utterances are contained in the Preface,[***] and yet there is but very little in the way of direct statement of theory upon which to base a consideration of the poet's practice in this particular case. Dryden, too, has carefully forestalled unfavorable criticism arising from a comparison of this drama with that which he has stated as essential to the composition of a good comedy, by denying that he has either the taste or the talent for this branch of dramatic composition; and yet an examination and criticism of this play cannot be omitted,

---

[*] Edition, l. c., p. 102.
[**] But compare Scott's remarks in his Life of Dryden (Ed., Vol. I, pp. 90, 91) and Jahrbuch der deutschen Shakespeare-Gesellschaft IV, p. 11—18 (article by Delius, who seems to ascribe the greater part to Dryden) and also pp. 152, 153 (Elze, in an article on Davenant); Rosebund, in a Halle Dissertation of 1882, "Dryden als Shakespearebearbeiter", brings nothing new on this point.
[***] vide Part First, § IV, of this paper.

and may possibly prove capable of affording us still
further insight into the difference between Dryden's two
capacities of critic and author.

A strict observance of the "unities" is neglected,
except that of *time;* the whole action occuring during
"the last evening of the carnival". The *place* is indicated
only in two cases; Act I, Scene II, "a chapel", and Act IV,
Scene II, "a garden"; although judging from allusions
in the play, the place of action is, besides, partly in an
apartment, partly in a street or square. The comedy
is written throughout in prose, with the exception of
one couplet at the end of each act, and about 20 lines
in blank-verse at the very beginning. A reason for
this latter is hardly apparent, unless we proceed upon
the hypothesis that it was Dryden's original intention
to write a part of the drama in this meter, but that
he soon abandoned it in favor of the more suitable
prose. In the course of the play (seemingly accidental)
are three or four isolated lines of blank-verse. The
plot is so full of intrigue as to be quite complicated, and
the unraveling comes only in the fifth act. The distinction
between comedy and farce is well observed, except in
the scenes in which the mock astrologer plays his rôle
of deception; for these scenes border on the farthest
verge of high improbability and should, therefore, find
their proper place in farce. In his Preface,* Dryden
considers that many of the comedies of his day (his
own and this particular play not excepted) are "too
much allied to farce", which he attributes to their being
translations from the French. And yet notwithstanding
the source, this drama as a whole contains but little
(outside of the scenes mentioned above) which could not
be considered as proper to comedy. Perhaps these
exceptions are to be excused by Dryden's stated preference
for "the mixed way of comedy, neither all wit, nor all
humour, but the result of both." As regards the *wit*
in the play, it may be said that Dryden has distinguished
between the different qualities of it in the different

* Edition, l. c., p. 242.

characters with some success. We certainly see "the imperfections of human nature" in the persons of the garrulous and credulous Don Alonzo and of the would-be fashionable Donna Aurelia; whether or not "the humours, adventures, and designs are such as are to be found and met with in the world" is a matter of grave doubt: Besides the improbable scenes with the mock astrologer I refer only to the flirtation in the chapel (Act I Scene II) which is both unreal and unseemly. But these improbabilities and unrealities (of which further examples in this play are not wanting) can be laid to the blame of the whole *genre* of Spanish intrigue plays, which at that time formed (through the medium of the French, in most cases) the principal source for the plots of English comedy. In fact, this drama is but ill adapted for a comparison of the way in which Dryden wrote comedy with his ideas of how it should be written, since it is not a piece upon which he prided himself (nor are his remarks on this subject to be considered in the same light as that affected modesty which is so obtrusive in his Dedications) nor is it, with all his claims of having "heightened" the original plot, very much more than an adaptation (with additions, it is true) of a foreign play. To permit of an effective comparison between Dryden's comedies and those of Fletcher, Jonson and Beaumont (which he criticizes, on various grounds, in the Preface) with a view to establish the superiority or inferiority of Dryden and his manner of carrying out his own principles, he should have furnished us with a specimen of a more genuinely English production and one written with the intention of illustrating certain theories. I need however, only to call to mind what I have before stated, that Dryden first wrote his plays and then the theoretical or critical essays published with them; so that it can never be safely asserted that the play to which the essay is attached is intended as an illustration of the principles stated in its preface, especially as Dryden usually is careful to state that the particular play contains many faults. Of course, however, in these present considerations of the relations between his theory and practice we must judge him, in spite of his protests and assumed modesty, by his own standard.

Dryden again abandons that style of writing (comedy) which he so often declares distasteful and unpleasant to him and occupies himself with a higher style of tragedy, but seldom attempted in English literature—the religious drama—in his next production:

IX.

"Tyrannic Love, or *The Virgin Martyr;"* first printed in 1670 (Edition, Vol. III, p. 369, seq.)

The *verse* of this play is the heroic couplet throughout, occasionaly interrupted by broken lines. The quality of the verse is inferior to much of that in the foregoing dramas: although the lines scan well, as a rule, the fault of ending them with verbs is of frequent occurrence; in many cases that "judicious" ordering of words, upon which Dryden insists (in passages which I have before quoted) being altogether absent. The Preface to the play states, however, that "the equality of numbers is not everywhere observed"—the reasons for this being partly haste, and partly because Dryden "would not have his sense a slave to syllables."

The Preface* claims for the play that "the scenes are everywhere unbroken, and the unities of place and time more exactly kept, than perhaps is requisite in a tragedy". The scenes are all laid with in a comparatively narrow limit, namely: "under the walls of Aquileia", in or near the camp of Maximin. It is also true that the scenes are unbroken, but this leads Dryden to commit the very absurdity for which he criticizes the French dramatists in the "Essay of Dramatic Poesy":** — "by tying themselves strictly to the unity of place, and un-

* Ed., l. c., p. 379.
** Arnold's Ed., p. 63, line 17 seq., and p. 64.

broken scenes, they are forced many times to omit some beauties which cannot be shown where the act began; but might, if the scene were interrupted, and the stage cleared for the persons to enter in another place; and therefore the French poets are often forced upon absurdities; for if the act begins in a chamber, all the persons in the play must have some business or other to come thither, or else they are not to be shown that act"; etc. An illustration of the absurdity which Dryden commits in following the rules he condemns is the fourth act of "Tyrannic Love." The scene is "An Indian Cave"* in which a conjuror summons certain spirits to answer the questions of Placidius regarding the success of Maximin's love for Catharine: This is an action fitting to the scene, and so also the appearance later on of Maximin himself might be considered. But utterly absurd is the arrival of Maximin's daughter, Valeria, whose dramatic "business" has nothing to do with magic, in such a place; and still more so the entrance of Berenice, Catharine and others; particularly as, with the arrival of each new character, the reason for the locality to be "An Indian Cave" disappears more and more completely, since the dialogue and action have become different from the time that the spirits and visions of the first hundred or so lines of the act have left the scene.** The same absurdity is also present (when perhaps in less degree)

---

* In itself a topographical absurdity! but see Saintsbury's note (l, c., p. 419) for the only reasonable explanation.
** An explanation of the above, perhaps only apparent, "absurdity" could be found in the construction of the stage of that period. From the many directions in plays by Dryden, such as "the scene draws" or "the scene closes", we are justified in the inference that a part of the center of the set scene at the back was closed by a curtain, which was withdrawn and closed in such cases as would be indicated by the stage directions I have mentioned. In this particular case we have the stage direction, before the entrance of Maximim, "the scene closes." Possibly the "Indian Cave" was represented as behind this curtain, so that after it was again drawn together, the scene would be the camp or pavilion of the other acts. But if we adopt this explanation, then it is not strictly true that the scenes are unbroken throughout the play.

in the other acts; for no matter whether the locality
indicated is "The Camp" or "The Royal Pavilion", all the
characters of the play come thither. Indeed, were it not
for the introduction of the incantation scene (one of the
weakest passages in the whole drama, by-the-way) the
place could have remained unchanged throughout the
entire drama, which would thereby have become still
more regular; for (with the exception just noted) the
dramatic "business" could have transpired as well in one
locality as another, and the fith act is without any indication of place whatever. The *time* is also brought into
very narrow limits—possibly only one day, but certainly
not more than two are required for the whole action.
Dryden might, with advantage, considering that "the
design is weighty, and the persons great", have allowed
more time; especially as this would not have been in-
consistent with his own expressed ideas on this point.
Dryden makes no statement in the preface to this play
regarding the presence of under-plots, although there
are at least two of these;* which feature alone is a
departure from the boasted regularity of the drama, (since
it is a neglect of the unity of action) although in harmony with Dryden's personal taste, as expressed in "The
Essay of Dramatic Poesy". Nor can it be said that
"the unity of action is sufficiently preserved" by making
"all the imperfect actions conducing to the main design".**
The main plot of the play is the love of Maximin to
St. Catharine and her martyrdom in consequence of her
refusal to comply with his desires; the under-plots and
"by-concernments",*** stand in no, or in only a distant,
relation to this main design. The "decorum of the stage"
is also violated, since the death of three of the principal

---

* The love of Porphyrius to Berenice and of Placidus to
Valeria; as a third might be added, the love of Valeria to
Porphyrius.
** Arnold, "Essay"; p. 57, line 15, seq.
*** One of these may possibly be an exception to my statement; namely the conversion of certain characters to Christianity
by the force of St. Catharine's words and example; since this,
perhaps, by increasing Maximin's anger, hastens and heightens the
catastrophe.

characters as well as certain "combats" are represented.
Nor will Dryden entirely deprive bis countrymen of
others of those "objects of horrour" which they so love
(according to the Essay),* for we are given a sight of
the torture-wheel and of a gallows; though he does not
gratify his audience by a use of these instruments in
the open scene (as in "The Indian Emperor", and later
in "Amboyna") and, besides, narrates the execution of
St. Catharine and her mother.

In view of the above examination we come to the
conclusion that "Tyannic Love" is neither an entirely
"correct" or "regulaɪ" play (according to the French
standard) nor are those departures from regularity which
Dryden had advocated up to this time, carried out;
This play forms, therefore, a good illustration of the
lack of any very close connection between theory and
praxis in Dryden's dramatic activity.

With regard to the avowed purpose of this drama
— "to second the precepts of religion" by "lively images
of piety, adorned by action"—we must give Dryden
credit for an honest attempt in this line, as embodied
in the person of St. Catharine, and for as powerful a
contrast to her as could be wished in the character of
Maximin. We may be allowed to doubt whether the
"precepts and examples of piety" had as much effect
upon a Restoration audience as the incantation scene
in the fourth act, and the curiosity to see how well
Nell Gwyn (Valeria) could act a serious part; It is safe
to conclude that the extremely worldly tone of the
Epilogue which this actress spoke removed any lingering
feeling in the minds of the spectators that the theatre
had been used as an aid to the pulpit.

In Dryden's next dramatic production we find him
fairly launched upon the sea of the heroic tragedy.
I refer to:

* Arnold, l. c., p. 61, line 1, seq.

X.

*"Almanzor and Almahide, or The Conquest of Granada
by the Spaniards;"* first published in 1672, (Edition Vol. IV,
p. 1, seq.)

This drama is an heroic tragedy of a pronounced
type and in every detail of form, action and characterization, and on this account is an examination of its
structure and technique of considerable interest. For
an analysis of the complicated ten-act plot (although
divided into two parts of five acts each, neither is in
itself complete) I refer to pp. 46—51 of Saintsbury's
"Life" in the "English Men of Letters Series", repeated
in the Edition, l. c. pp. 7—10. The peculiarly heroic
elements are treated in Holzhausen's essay, particularly
in Theil II, §§ 3 & 4;* and in this connection it may
be said at once that the characters are thoroughly in
keeping with those which Dryden considers (in the
Preface to the First Part**) as fitting and proper for
heroic plays. All the bombastic absurdities and exaggerated notions of "love and honour" (the two mainsprings
of the whole heroic species) are defended by Dryden,
in his analysis of Almanzor and the comparison between
him and other heroes (in the above mentioned Preface)
in such a style, that we can only say: In this point
Dryden shows no deviations between theory and praxis.
So we have to hold ourselves principally to such theories
as had been advanced by him in former essays and not
revoked or reconsidered in the two ("Of Heroic Plays",
and "Defence of the Epilogue") which were published together with this play. In the opening words of the
"Essay on Heroic Plays", Dryden regards the question
of the rhymed couplet as being definitely settled,***

* Englische Studien, Band XV.
** vide Part First, § VI, of this paper.
*** "Whether heroic verse ought to be admitted into serious
plays is not now to be disputed: it is already in possession of
the stage." Ed., l. c., p. 19.

and so this play is naturally rhymed throughout, with the exception of the frequently employed broken lines. Scenes of "argumentation or discourse," and of repartee, are, as might be expected, numerous in a play which, like this, is made up so largely of conflicts between love and honor, and the pleadings of a rejected or unrequited passion; and such scenes are (for this style of drama) exceedingly effective—owing, no doubt, largely to the rhyme alone.* As regards the unity of *place:* the scene does not overstep the limits of the Moorish Kingdom, and is, in fact, limited to the capital of Granada and its immediate surroundings. In the whole of the first part there is, however, but one indication of place; namely, in Act V, Scene II, "under the walls of the Albayzyn." For Act I, Part I we can suppose, with great probability judging from the character of the action, that the place is some street or open square in the city. Acts III and IV of Part I must be supposed to take place in some apartment (probably of the Albayzyn) as can be seen by the stage directions on pp. 68, 69, 81, 85 and 88 of the Edition, in which entrances through doors are distinctly mentioned. In the second part the place is indicated throughout, with two exceptions, namely; Act IV, Scene I, and Act V, Scene I. For the first of these we may suppose with reason the Alhambra to be the scene of action, since Abenamar enters and converses with Selin "bound"; the latter being, according to Act III, Scene II (p. 165) — "a prisoner to his greatest foe:

Kept with strong guards in the Alhambra tower."

It is not easy to determine the locality of the first scene of Act V, which consists in fact only of a few lines of monologue and dialogue with no action except the bringing in of Abdelmelech "guarded". Perhaps the most reasonable conclusion is that no particular scene was intended by the author, but that the few words are spoken in front of a curtain which afterwards is withdrawn and

---

* See, for one instance among many, Act II, Sc. I, of Part 1, the dialogues between Abdalla and Lyndaraxa, and Abdalla and Zulema.

discloses Scene II; which, as it is "filled with spectators" and contains "a scaffold hung with black" would require most of the disposable stage room: In other words, Scene I Act V, Part II is a "carpenter scene". In both parts the indications of place, when such are found at all, are usually quite general, and principally "the Alhambra" or "the Albayzyn". * The *time* of Part I is within the limits of one day. The action of Part II begins upon the following day, as we can surmise from Boab· delin's words (Act V, Part I, p. 115) after he has been successful in routing his enemies—"Let war and vengeance be to-morrow's care",—and by the bringing in of Osmyn and Benzayda as captives in Act I Part II,

---

* Notwithstanding the advancement in scenery and decorations of the English stage at the period of the Restoration, somewhat of the old Shakespearian naïveté and simplicity, as regards the representation of locality, must have remained. This can be seen in many of the Restoration dramas and not for the least part in the "Conquest of Granada", which must have been performed on a stage not unlike the present *Shakespeare-Bühne* in Munich. Such a stage would excuse the absence of definite directions as to locality in the drama as printed; since, where no scene at all is indicated, the reader of that time would put it at once, in nearly every case, in front of that curtain of which I have spoken in the note on p. 49; this arrangement explains also, perhaps, the first scene of Act V, Part II of this play. So, too, could we explain an apparent oversight of Dryden's in Scene II, Act V, Part II, all of which (according to the printed text, since no change of scene is indicated) transpires in the Vivarambla place. But on p. 214, l. c., Abdelmelech announces that the Spaniards have gained possession of this place, although they have not, as yet, entered upon the scene. The stage-direction for Scene II is: "The Scene changes to the Vivarambla", etc., and if we assume that this means only that the curtain at the rear has been withdrawn and is closed again after the trial by combat (which is to decide the question of Almahides conjugal fidelity) at the words : (l. c., p. 207) "The judges rise from their seats — — — — — they all go off", the seeming incongruity is clear enough. It may also be mentioned, in this connection, that on the rear wall of the Restoration Stage, as well as in Shakespeare's time, there was a balcony, which plays an important part in more than one of Dryden's dramas: for instance in this play, Act V, Scene II (l. c., p. 213) and in "The Indian Emperor", Act V, Scene II (Vol. III p. 403, seq.). Compare Gaedertz: Zur Kenntniss der altenglischen Bühne, Bremen, 1888, p. 15.

who had fled from the city in Scene I, Act V, Part I.
The *time* of this second part does not exceed 24 hours:
need not, in fact, exceed twelve: The unity of *action* is
quite neglected, for there are two or three "underplots
and by-concernments" beside the principal action; though
it must be admitted that these all stand in close connection
to the "main design" and "contribute (in greater or
less degree) to it."

The "decorum of the stage" suffers badly indeed,
inasmuch as we find many combats and tumults, as
well as the deaths of several of the principal characters, represented. On the whole, it must be concluded
regarding this play, as I have said above concerning
"Tyrannic Love", that it is neither "regular" according
to the French standard (although two of the unities are
strictly observed), nor is it written entirely after the
principles laid down by Dryden himself in the essays,
etc., written up to this date. But as an example of an
heroic drama it is one of the very best of its class.

An examination of this play with reference to the
assertions made in the Epilogue to the 2d part, which
are enlarged upon in the "Defence of the Epilogue",
namely: "that the language, wit, and conversation of
our age, are improved and refined above the last", would
certainly show up Dryden as being guilty of some of
the very faults for which he criticizes Jonson, Shakespeare
and Fletcher. To mention but one—it may be questimed
whether it is not as great an absurdity for Abdalla to
draw a simile from" Circe's isle", and for Lyndaraxa to
exclaim: "We have already passed the Rubicon" (to say
nothing of various other classical allusions in the mouths
of Moors of the 15" century) as for Demetrius (in Jonson's
"Humorous Lieutenant") to appear "with a pistol in his
hand, in the next age to Alexander the Great". It cannot
be denied, however, that there is a change, if not an
improvement and refinement, in the "language, wit and
conversation" of Dryden's plays, as compared with those
of his great predecessors; and that he has (and most
particularly in this drama) caught the style best adapted

to that court and nobility to which he attributes these
advances in taste above the former age.

Dryden's next play was:

XI.

"Marriage à la Mode"; published in 1673. (Edition,
Vol. IV, page 247, seq.)

Although the title-page calls this "A Comedy", it
contains also a serious plot, and therefore might properly
be classed as "Tragi-Comedy". The form is a mixture
of prose, blank-verse and rhymed couplets; the two
latter being employed in the serious and some of the
love-making scenes without apparent discrimination—
one of those "scenes of argumentation or discourse"
which Dryden considered so particularly adapted to be
clothed in rhyme (Act II, p. 288—293, l. c.) is in blank
verse. The ends of all acts, and of Sc. I Act III and
IV, Act IV are marked by one or more rhymed couplets.
The unity of *action* is broken by the double plot. The
unity of *place* is fairly observed according to Dryden's
own standard, since the action takes place throughout
in Syracuse, although the scene is indicated but twice
in the play; namely Act I, "Walks near the Court";
and Scene IV, Act IV "An Eating-house". Although a
modern audience would require a change of locality,
in order to avoid an inconsistency occasioned by causing
so many events to transpire in the same place, the
construction of the stage of Dryden's time (see notes
on pp. 49 and 54) which left the actual scene so
much to the imagination of the spectator must be taken
into account as an explanation. If we were to assume,
however, that Dryden intended the entire action (with
the exception of the scene which he expressly indicates
as in an eating-house) to transpire in the "Walks near
the Court" we would be led into as great absurdities
as he himself condemns (because of "unbroken-scenes")
in the French; since assignations, a masquerade and

grave affairs of state would have all but the one scene
as a background. One is justified in supposing that the
scenic decorations for ordinary comedy were of extreme,
almost naive simplicity,* however magnificent they
may have been in the heroic dramas. The duration of
the *time* is not less than two days, although it cannot
be determined with any great exactness. This is a
reversion of the rule laid down by Dryden (in the
"Defence of the Essay") if we take the "Conquest of
Granada" as a comparison, for the time of each part of
this latter is confined within the "classical" limits and
to "Marriage à la Mode" is allowed a much greater
space; although, because of the weight of design and
action and the importance of the characters represented,
a tragedy may, according to Dryden, cover a larger
imaginary space of time than a comedy. The only critical
essay written by Dryden, up to this time, which has a
direct bearing upon comedy was the preface to "An
Evening's Love"** and judging "Marriage à la Mode"
by what is said in that place we find, first of all, that
Dryden has here well distinguished between comedy
and farce since there are no "forced humours and unnatural events", and that the whole of the comic action
is strictly in character. Nor are "the follies of particular
persons" represented, but rather such as belong to different
classes of humanity and that, too, in a way which must
have seemed very real to the spectators of Dryden's
time. The characters are certainly "well chosen" and
kept "distant from interfering with each other", for
each is distinctly different in its own kind, nor are the
"ornaments of wit" wanting. Even in the repartee—
"the greatest grace of comedy"—Dryden has been careful
to avoid "the superfluity and waste of wit" which he
blames in Shakespeare and Fletcher, and has skillfully
characterized the particular quality of wit of each person.

---

* So the "Eating-house" in this play could have been sufficiently characterized by the "Bottles of Wine" and the "Table"
mentioned in the stage directions, p. 330, l. c.
** vide Part I, § IV of this paper.

Dryden's next drama was also a comedy:

XII.

"The Assignation, or Love in a Nunnery"; published in 1673 (Edition, Vol. IV, p. 365, seq.) which met with no great success. The form is prose throughout, except for some lines of rather indifferent blank-verse (particularly in the fifth act) and rhymed couplets at the end of each act. The *place* is here exactly indicated for nearly every scene; and where not, the action takes place in the locality named in the last preceding stage-direction. The scene is limited to the city of Rome; and, especially, to the Nunnery "Torre di Specchi". The *time* must be about three days, from indications in the dialogue. The unity of *action* is violated, since there are at least two plots, each of them of nearly equal importance. The same favorable judgment regarding the essential features of comedy cannot be passed here as upon the last-mentioned drama, though there is, at least, an avoidance of farcial elements.*

XIII.

„*The State of Innocence and Fall of Man*", published in 1674 (Editon, Vol. V, p. 93, seq.) is a dramatization of Milton's "Paradise Lost", and was not intended for representation. Indeed a representation would have been hardly possible, even with the aid of all the advances in stage-machinery which the Restoration

---

* It may be excused if I pass over with but few words— "*Amboyna*, or *The Cruelties of the Dutch to the English Merchants*, a Tragedy" published 1673 (Edition, Vol. V, p. 1, seq.); called by Scott (l. c., p. 3) "the worst production which Dryden ever wrote". An entire absence of artistic purpose in this piece with a purely political tendency, renders an examination of its technique almost superfluous.

had introduced. From the very nature of this so-called "opera" an application of any of Dryden's theories upon technique is hardly feasible; eyen the "Apology, for Heroic Poetry and Poetic Licence" prefixed to it, gives no points upon which to base such a consideration. The piece is rhymed throughout.

XIV.

Once more, and for the last time our author takes up the heroic pen in "Aureng-Zebe"; published in 1676 (Edition, Vol. V, p. 179, seq.) and herewith furnishes one of the best proofs that "The Rehearsal", did not, as Hettner * claims, put a sudden end to this style of drama, for we have here still all the familiar features of rhymed couplets and exaggerated notions of love and honor. In the Dedication, however, Dryden expresses (l. c., p. 195) an evidently genuine desire to abandon heroic verse, and the Prologue (l. c., p. 20) makes the confession that the author —

"Grows weary of his long-loved mistress, Rhyme."
"Aureng-Zebe" is, however, (with the exception of occasional "broken lines", and seven lines in blank-verse on page 242 & 245 l. c.) rhymed throughout;

---

* "Geschichte der englischen Literatur im 18. Jahrhundert", Braunschweig 1881, p. 90—"Die gereimte heroische Tragödie war für immer verloren — — — — Der Schlag war tödlich gewesen." But compare with this Saintsbury's remarks in his Life of Dryden ("English Men of Letters") page 52; Ward, History of English Dramatic Literature, Vol. II, p. 510, and Holzhausen l. c. X.III, p. 434. The last-named has undoubtedly stated the effect of this clever parody most clearly of all. I may take it for granted that the incidents connected with the production of "The Rehearsal", the names of its authors, etc., are sufficiently well known by all students of English literature of that period to make repetition here unnecessary. I need only to refer (among other sources of information) to Hettner (l. c, pp. 89 and 90) and, particularly, to Scott, Life of Dryden, Edition, Vol. I, pp. 113—121.

although, as Scott points out in the Introduction (l. c., pp. 182 & 185) the "heroic" character of the verse is very much moderated.

Another line in the Prologue states that the author "presumes" this play "the most correct of his," but it cannot be called entirely correct, since (in the first place) the unity of *action* is absent. There are as many pairs of lovers, with their various intrigues, as in any of Dryden's earlier heroic dramas: so, for instance the loves of Aureng-Zebe and Indamora (the main plot), then the passion of Nourmahal for Aureng-Zebe, of the Emperor and Morat for Indamora, and one or two other cases of unrequited affection. It cannot be denied, however, that these side-issues stand in very close connection to the main plot and contribute to the final catastrophe. It is worthy of mention, too, that although a further lack of "correctness" consists in the prominence of several of the secondary persons, these are drawn and characterized with much greater carefulness and distinctness than in any earlier tragedy of our author. As regards the unity of *place*, the drama is entirely correct so far as can be judged from the printed text. No changes of scene whatever are indicated, except the general locality: Agra. As to whether the action takes place in an apartment or in some street or open square, we are left in doubt. The "absurdity" which Dryden finds in the French plays would obtain in this, also; unless we are to suppose that, in the representation, changes of scene were effected which are not given in the text. The imaginary *time* of this play does not exceed one day; the action ending late at night of the same day on which it begins. Although but little fighting takes place by open scene, a sufficient number of deaths are represented to disturb the "decorum" of the stage. Altogether, however, this drama distinguishes itself from others of the heroic stamp by its great moderation, although it has no more claim to be called "regular" or "correct" than "The Conquest of Granada".

XV.

Dryden's next play was another remodelling of Shakespeare, namely; *"All for Love, or the World well Lost"*, published 1678 (Edition, Vol. V, p. 305, seq.) — an adaptation of "Antony and Cleopatra". If in the Dedication and Prologue to "Aureng-Zebe" our author shows himself evidently weary of rhymed verse, he would attribute the rhymlessness of this play simply to his wish to follow Shakespeare more closely; for he does "not condemn his former way" but blank-verse is "more proper to his present purpose". "Aureng-Zebe" was, however, his last play rhymed throughout, and we may properly conclude that Dryden was convinced of the necessity of a change of form; either because rhyme was out of favor through the success of "The Rehearsal", which made sport of the whole heroic style, or (as he states in the Dedication to the "Essay of Dramatic Poesy".)* because he found "the way of writing plays in verse troublesome and slow." The exact reason for Dryden's abandoning a form of verse which he had defended so strongly is not easy to find, nor do his own statements upon the subject help us very much, since they are somewhat at variance with one another. It is hardly possible that an author who wrote so much and so easily in rhymed verse is in earnest when he calls himself "the Sisyphus of the Stage", or finds rhyming "troublesome and slow"; Nor can it be his thorough conviction that — "Passion's too fierce to be in fetters bound" or he would have considered twice before enchaining the verse of "Aureng-Zebe" with such "fetters"; Least of all is "The Rehearsal" entirely the cause of the change; for Dryden ignored (or affected to ignore) this attack upon his work and his personality. Though each one of these reasons may have had its share in bringing about the change, no single element is alone responsible for it.

---

* Arnold, Edition, p. 2, line 4, seq.

Besides all this, it is beyond dispute that Dryden, from the very beginning of his dramatic career, had more or less respect for, and sympathy with, the elder English dramatists, probably including even the form in which they wrote; but in the conflict between this sentiment of veneration on the one hand, and the Gallicized taste of the court as well as the number of French "authorities" on the other, the style of composition most in conformity with this second party triumphed, for a while at least. I am inclined, in fact, to attribute the abandoning of rhyme quite as much to the "secret shame" which Dryden says, in the Prologue to "Aureng-Zebe" invaded "his breast at Shakespeare's sacred name" as to any other assignable reason. Outside of the question of rhyme Dryden's opinions on certain points here, at the time of composing "All for Love", were practically unchanged, judging from the Preface; for although he brings to notice the regularity of the drama, he still considers such a strict observance of the unities "more than the English theatre requires", and that the ancient models are "too little for English tragedy." An examination of the play as regards technique seems hardly necessary, since Dryden himself gives all that is important upon this point in the Preface. For a comparison with Shakespeare's drama, I refer to Rosbund's essay, "Dryden als Shakespearebearbeiter", Halle 1882; and Scott's Introduction, l. c., pp. 307—313.

The next play in order is:

XVI.

"Limberham, the Kind Keeper"; a Comedy, published in 1678. (Edition, Vol. VI, p. 1, seq.)

Although one of Dryden's best comedies, as far as regards structure and dialogue, this play was not successful. The reason is not clear, but can hardly lie in its extreme indecency, since an audience of the

Restoration period would scarcely make very serious objections to it on that score. The form is prose throughout; even the rhymed couplets at the close of the acts failing, except at the very end of the play. It is worthy of remark that the scenes of repartee (particularly between Woodall and Mistress Pleasance) seem quite as lively and telling in this form as if written in rhymed verse. The action is fairly one, since it all turns upon the gallant adventures of the rake Woodall, and his final surrender to the conjugal yoke. The imaginary *time* of the action is between two and three days. The unity of *place* is almost strictly observed, since the locality is "a lodging-house", and all the scenes transpire in some room of the house or in the garden belonging to it. The comedy is never farcial, and the wit (though extremely broad, to say the least) is well adapted to each person indulging in it. The characters are certainly "well-drawn and kept distant from interfering with each other": they give the impression of being taken from life * in all particulars. Otherwise this drama does not call for especial remark in this place, since Dryden's attitude towards comedy had not undergone, up to this time, any change — at least as expressed in any theorizing upon the technique of this branch of dramatic art. From what I have said above it can be seen, however, that "Limberham" shows a fair amount of consistency to the theories and criticism already expressed by Dryden.

XVII.

"*Œdipus*", a Tragedy, published in 1679; (Edition, Vol. VI, p. 121, seq.) was the joint work of Dryden and Lee. Noticeable in the short Preface (l. c., p. 133) is Dryden's defence of the "underplot of second persons"

---

* Vide Scott's introduction; l. c., p. 1.

on the ground that "custom has obtained" that this should be so; to which he adds; "Perhaps, after all, if we could think so, the ancient method, as it is the easiest, is also the most natural, and the best. For variety, as it is managed, is too often subject to breed distraction; and while we would please too many ways, for want of art in the conduct, we please in none." Tentatively and cautiously as Dryden here expresses himself, it is easy to recognize a desire for greater simplicity and "regularity" than had been his practice in tragedy up to this time, or his theory as expressed in the "Essay of Dramatic Poesy".* In some other particulars, however, "Œdipus" (at least) shows no advance towards better taste; since, as Scott well remarks in the Introduction (1. c., p. 128), there is no English play "more determinedly bloody in its progress and conclusion. — — — — Of all the persons of the drama scarce one survives the fifth act. — — — — The play which begins with a pestilence, concludes with a massacre." The rant and bombast of certain scenes is also quite as bad as anything which had been produced up to that time. But, regarding both these points, we must not forget that Dryden is not the sole author of the drama, and that a good deal of the blame, as regards both plan and execution, might well be attributed to his collaborateur, Lee. This fact of a joint authorship also precludes the necessity for an examination of this play similar to that to which the foregoing have been subjected. It may be remarked, however, that the form is blank-verse, except for the rhymes of the incantation scene in the third act and the couplets terminating each act.

XVIII.

Dryden again devotes himself to Shakespeare in his next play, *"Troilus and Cressida, or Truth Found too Late"*; published in 1679. (Ed., Vol. VI, p. 241, seq.)

---

* Vide Arnold's Ed., pp. 56, 57 & 59.

What "improvements" he has made upon his great model are recorded by Dryden himself in the Preface, and by Scott in the Introduction to this play. An examination of this play in comparison with the principles laid down in the essay "On the Grounds of Criticism in Tragedy",* would occupy too much time and space; but it may be said, in general, that the wicked are punished in accordance with the demands of dramatic justice as stated in that place; that the "manners" are treated in harmony with the rules there promulgated and that the "unities" are as strictly observed as the model upon which this adaptation is founded would allow. Dryden had broken once for all with rhyme, so it is not surprising that this play contains none, except the customary couplets at the ends of the acts. Among other particulars we note the great advance made towards simplicity of style as compared with the heroic dramas; so, for instance, in the absence of bombast and rant.

XIX.

The remaining dramas of Dryden are, in the chronological order of their publication, the following:

1) *"The Spanish Friar, or The Double Discovery"*, a Tragi-Comedy; published in 1681. (Ed., Vol. VI, p. 393, seq.)

2) *"The Duke of Guise"*, a Tragedy (written in conjunction with Lee); published in 1685. (Ed., Vol. VII, p. 1, seq.)

3) *"Albion and Albanius"*, an Opera; published in 1685. (Ed., Vol. VII, p. 221, seq.)

---

* Vide the analysis in Part I, § IX of this paper.

4) *"Don Sebastian"*, a Tragedy; published in 1690. (Ed., Vol. VII, p. 285, seq.)

5) *"Amphitryon, or The Two Sosias"*, a Comedy; published in 1690. (Edition, Vol. VIII, p. 1, seq.)

6) *„King Arthur, or The British Worthy"*, a Dramatic Opera; published in 1691. (Ed., Vol. VIII, p. 123, seq.)

7) *"Cleomenes. The Spartan Hero"*, a Tragedy; published in 1692. (Ed., Vol. VIII, p. 203, seq.)

8) *"Love Triumphant, or Nature will Prevail"*, a Tragi-Comedy; published 1693—94. (Edition, Vol. VIII, p. 365, seq.)

— The evidence in favor of Dryden's authorship for the two doubtful plays, "The Mall" and "The Mistaken Husband", included by Saintsbury in his Edition (Vol. VIII), is by no means sufficiently conclusive; on which account I omit any consideration of them here. —

It is unnecessary to examine these eight dramas with the same attention which I have devoted to the foregoing, since Dryden's dramatic technique underwent no important changes after this time, and the theories which he utters after "The Grounds of Criticism in Tragedy" are either a repetition of such as he had before promulgated or merely a more definite declaration of his change of taste in some particulars. So (as regards this latter point) he bids a final farewell to bombast in the Dedication to *"The Spanish Friar"*,* and acknowledges the sins he had committed in that direction. His tragedies are from this time on (and had been, in fact, since "Aureng-Zebe") of a much calmer nature in both action and dialogue, with the exception of the bloodiness of "Œdipus". The Preface to *"Don*

---

* Vide Part First, § X, of this paper.

Sebastian",* in its statements regarding ‧love and honour", only confirms the praxis of his latter days in avoiding the ‧heroic" conflicts between these two motives. The attitude which he should observe towards the "unities" is as great a question with him in both the theory and praxis of these latter days as it ever had been. If he writes a tragedy without a comic underplot (*"Cleomenes"*) he defends this as being ‧the true way"; but he excuses a double plot (*"The Spanish Friar"* and *"Love Triumphant"*) by ‧the pleasure of variety" or the ‧genius of the English". The other unities (besides that of action) are treated as suits his particular convenience (*"Don Sebastian"*, *"Cleomenes"* and *"Love Triumphant"*) though not without explanation or excuse in the accompanying dedication or preface.

* Vide Part First, § XII, of this paper.

The whole question of the relation existing between Dryden's dramatic theory and his praxis may be summed up in the following sentences: Dryden evinces on the one side, the greatest veneration for the authority of the "Ancients" and the French Classicists (which finds its highest expression in "The Grounds of Criticism in Tragedy"); and on the other side, the desire to please the court and public; which latter feature is strengthened by the fact (now undisputed) that his circumstances were seldom so good that authorship was not necessary as a means of existence. The expressed admiration and attempted imitation of Shakespeare in the last 25 years or so of his dramatic career, bring him more or less into conflict with the regularity demanded by Aristotle, but yet from first to last (excepting in "The Grounds of Criticism in Tragedy") Dryden has been an advocate of a certain latitude in the observance of the unities. But still with what pride he points out the fact when he has written a play in which the unities are almost exactly observed (as in "*Tyrannic Love*," or "*Aureng-Zebe*") and particularly does he consider it a great merit on his part to have made some of Shakespeare's plays more "regular". On the whole, I fail to discover any such intimate connection between theory and praxis in Dryden's dramatic authorship as might reasonably be expected. Nowhere does he say; "thus and thus shall be written" and then follow up these exact lines. The changes in both theory and praxis after the appearance of "*Aureng-Zebe*" (notably in the abandonment of rhyme) make the impression of being made to suit the taste of his audiences first, and accounted for by critical dicta afterwards: — the aban-

doning of rhyme being (as he would give us to understand in the Prologue to „*Aureng-Zebe*" and the Preface
to the 2" Edition of the "Essay of Dramatic Poesy")
quite as much because it was "troublesome and slow"
as for any other reason. The heroic plays seem to
show the greatest consistency between theory and
practice. The heroic verse had been commended on
more than one occasion by Dryden, even from the time
of the Dedication to "*The Rival-Ladies*", and the other
characteristic features of the heroic style of drama are
treated in full in the "Essay of Heroic Plays", and occur
in all the heroic tragedies written by Dryden. Yet even
here one or two notable examples had been produced
before our author laid down his theories for the whole
species. With this exception of the heroic tragedy,
where, it is true, visible coherence exists between theory
and praxis, I must, in conclusion, emphazise the following facts; A comparison of such statements of individual
opinion as are to be found in Dryden's essays, prefaces
and dedications regarding points of dramatic technique,
with his practice in dramatic composition, lead to the
discovery of a lack of any *exact* organic connection in
every particular between the two: An attempt to show
either a complete reconciliation between theory and
praxis or a complete divergence of each from the
other leads to no precise results: The dramas were in
nearly every instance (the exceptions being the heroic
tragedies and the Shakespeare adaptations) composed
according to the fancy of the poet or the demands of
the sources of the plots, without slavish adherence to
theory: The theoretical writings are only to be regarded,
first of all as essays upon the style and nature of
dramatic art in general; and, secondly, as written to
justify the author in the eyes of the public in regard
to his own dramas.

Vita.

I, George Stuart Collins, was born Sept. 25, 1862, in New Rochelle, State of New York, U. S. A. My first instruction I received from my Father, an evangelical pastor, and afterwards studied at private schools and the High School of Plainfield, New Jersey, from which last-named institution I graduated in 1881. An intended course of study at Columbia College, New York City, was prevented by long and frequent illnesses. In 1885 I came to Germany for the purpose of study, and was immatriculated at the University of Leipzig in the Winter Semester of 1885/86. Here I have since remained, and have attended during this time the lectures of the following professors and docents: Drs. Arndt, von Bahder, Biedermann, Ebert, Hildebrand, Hirt, Kögel, Körting, Lindner, Masius, Settegast, Sievers, Springer, Techmer, Windisch, Wülker, Wundt and Zarncke. I have also been, for several semesters, a member of the Deutsches Seminar, ausserordentliche Abtheilung, as well as, for one semester each, of the Gesellschaften of Profs. Ebert and Wülker. During the past year I have been engaged in lexicographic and literary labors. To Prof. Wülker I desire to express my thanks for many welcome words of advice.

L e i p z i g, May, 1892.